WATCH OUT,
Little
Narwhal!

Jane Riordan

Richard Watson

bookoli

It is quiet in the Arctic, but hear that call...

Who's that coming? It's **Narwhal Small!**

And here, with his tusk, it's **Narwhal Pa.**

And the unicorn of the sea, it's **Narwhal Ma.**

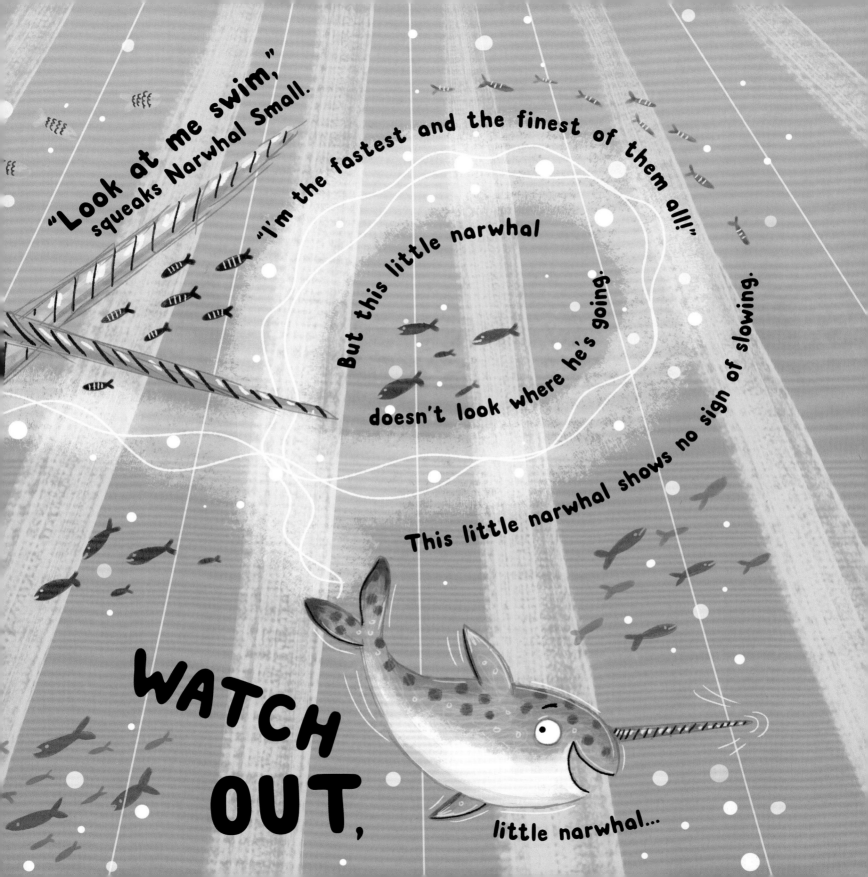

BUMP!

Poor Narwhal Small is completely stuck.
He's tangled in seaweed, what terrible luck!

"My silly tusk," says Narwhal Small. "It causes such trouble, it's no use at all."

But a friend **with tentacles** is here **to help**...

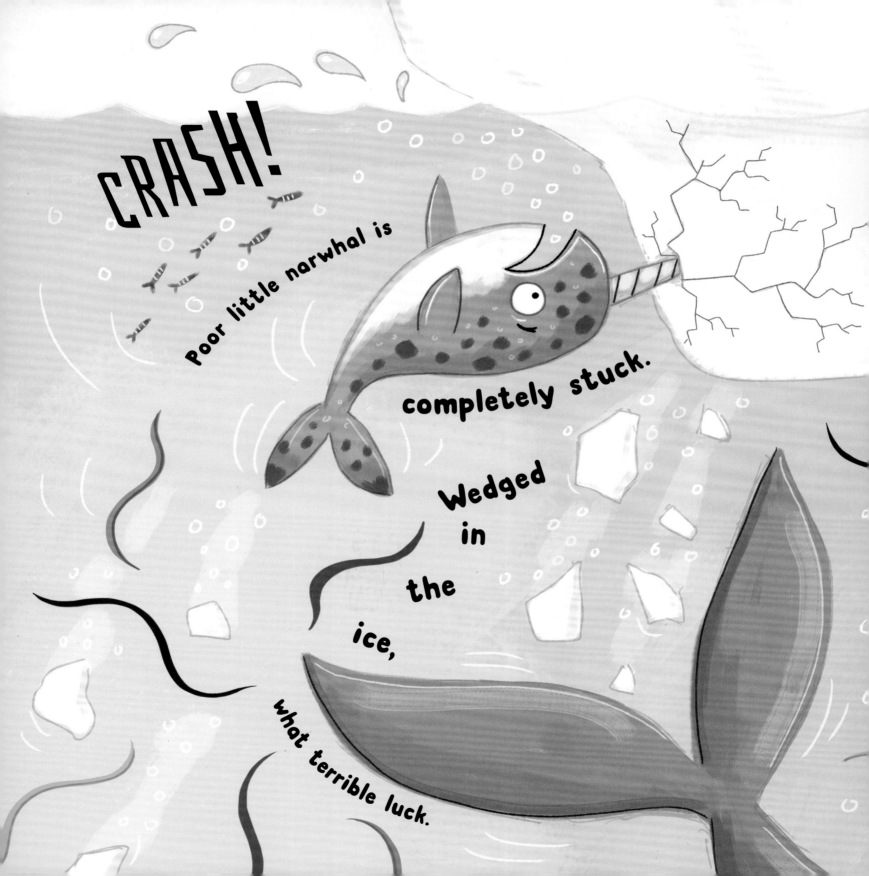

It's Polar Pete!

He stamps on the ice with a thud and a **thump**.

CRACK!

Small is free with one final jump.

"Look at me swim," squeaks Narwhal Small. "I'm the fastest and the finest of them all!"

But this little narwhal doesn't look where he's going.

This little narwhal shows no sign of slowing.

WATCH OUT, little narwhal!

BUMP!

Poor little narwhal is completely stuck.
His tusk deep in sand, what terrible luck.

It's Simi Seal!

She uses her snout to nuzzle in the sand,

soon Small is free, just as Simi had planned.

But Small is quiet now. Small seems sad.

He swims away slowly, back to his dad.

"I'd rather," he sighs, "have no tusk at all.

I hate being different," says Narwhal Small.

The next day Small and his Ma and Pa,
are invited to a party
that's not too far.
They arrive at the place,
what a sight meets their eyes!

A party just for Small,
what a surprise!

All the tiny creatures are waiting side by side,
then one asks, very shyly, if they can have a ride.

WHEEEEE!

"Look at us go," squeaks Narwhal Small.

"My tusk is useful after all!"

"I may be different, I may look strange, but it's special being different, and I wouldn't want to change. I love being just the way I am."

And with a flick of his tusk, away Small swam.